For Thomas and Danny Boy

With special thanks to Lucy

First published 2003 by Walker Books Ltd
87 Vauxhall Walk, London SE11 5HJ

2 4 6 8 10 9 7 5 3 1

© 2003 Flora McDonnell

The right of Flora McDonnell to be identified as
author/illustrator of this work has been asserted
by her in accordance with the
Copyright, Designs and Patents Act 1988

This book has been typeset in Golden Cockerel

Printed in China

British Library Cataloguing in Publication Data:
a catalogue record for this book is available
from the British Library

ISBN 0-7445-9672-6

Sparky

Flora McDonnell

WALKER BOOKS
AND SUBSIDIARIES
LONDON • BOSTON • SYDNEY

This is Sparky.

He has just arrived
at his new home.
Everything feels
a bit strange.

Mum comforts him.
"Mary is just coming,"
she says. "You'll have such
fun together."
Sparky wags his tail.
He likes Mum.
She makes him feel safe.

This is Mary.

She is so excited.

"Sparky!" she shouts.

Sparky is excited too.
He thinks Mary is probably
another kind of puppy.
It's love at first sight.
"Come on, Sparky!"
Mary says. "I'll show
you everything."

In her room Mary
puts on her favourite music.
Sparky likes it too.
"Let's dance, Sparky!"
Mary says.

Then Mary takes Sparky into the garden to dig for treasure in the sandpit. "Look how Sparky digs, Mum!" Mary calls.

"Follow me,
Sparky!"
Mary slides
down the slide.

Wheee!

Sparky
slides
down
after
her.

Sparky and Mary have tea together at Mary's table.
Sparky eats very fast.
He is so hungry.

Now it's Mary's bathtime.
But Sparky wants
to play tug-of-war.
"Let go, Sparky!"
Mary giggles.

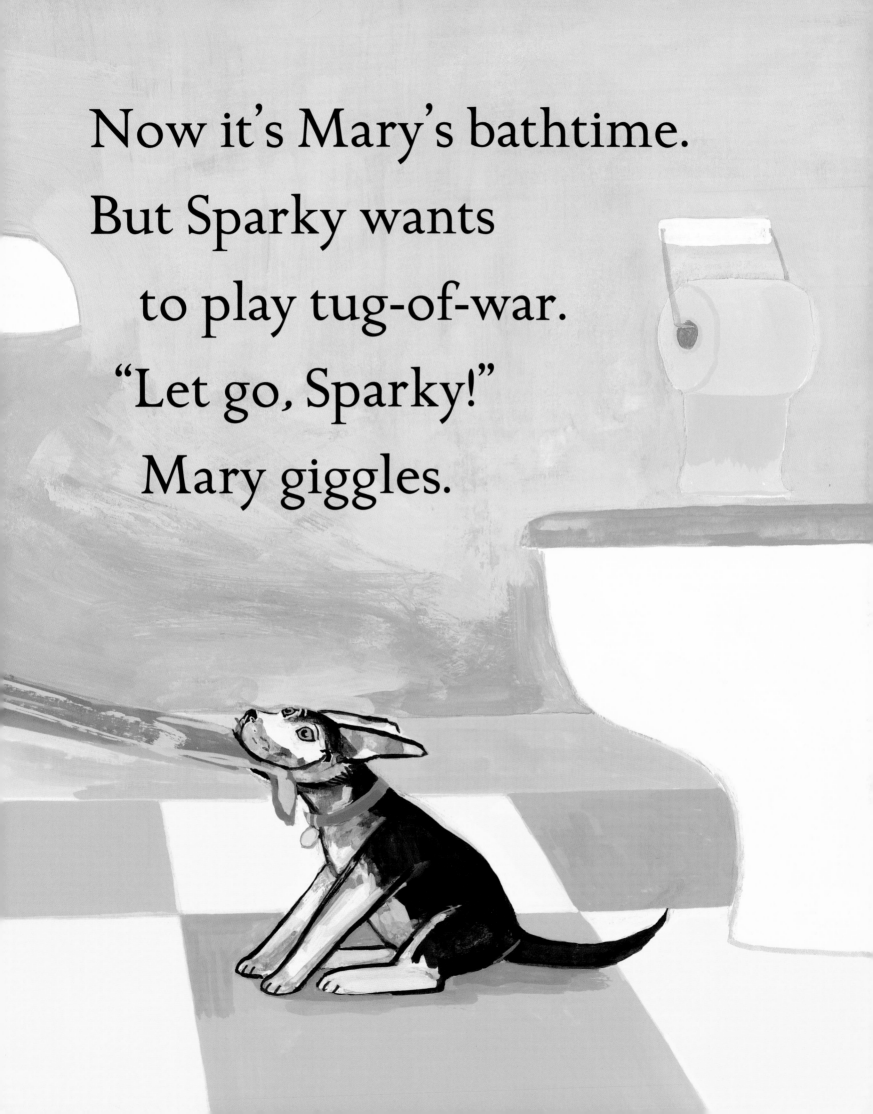

While Mary brushes
her teeth, Sparky tries
and tries to catch his tail.

He never can.

"Silly Sparky!"

Mary says.

Mary
bounces
on her
bed.

Sparky
bounces
too,
higher
and
higher.

Sssshh!

Goodnight, Mary!

Goodnight, Sparky!

What a lovely day it's been.